ISBN 1-877724-99-8
Library of Congress Catalog
Number is: 96-090545
Copyright 1997
Revised 1999

Freedom & Victory Publishing, Inc.
P.O. Box 2517
Stone Mountain, GA 30386

**Amanda's Poor Self-Image**

**Acknowledgment**

The author expresses her gratitude to all who have contributed to the writing, editing and publication of this book. Special thanks to The Great Intelligence, Zakiyyah Shumpert, Amanda Esther Aquino, Khyanna Pumphery, Jill Weckesser, Shahanna Mckenney, and my family.

Geraldine Shaheed

Illustrated by Amanda Esther Aquino

# I Will Learn About My Self-Image

*This book has been written for you to read either alone or with your family. Difficult words are marked by an asterisk (\*). The definitions of these words are shown at the bottom of the pages. If you would like to know more about these words, a GLOSSARY has been provided at the back of this book.*

*My picture or my family's picture*

*My name or my family's name:------------------------------*

# Amanda's Poor Self-Image

You are about to learn about
the concept of 'self-image' and how
you can develop a good self-image.
Self-image is a picture you have
of yourself in your mind's eye.
There are two types of self-image:
1) An unhealthy self-image.
2) A healthy, happy, and
beautiful self-image.

# Learning About Amanda's Poor Self-Image

Once upon a time, there was a young girl named Amanda Enis. She was a very sad little girl, both at home and at school. Her sister, Aiesha, and the children at school always found something wrong with her. They said her hair was too long, her nose was too short, her feet were too big, and her clothes were too old! Amanda developed a poor image of herself. Amanda had always visualized herself with a poor self-image, and because of this, she felt very sad and lonely.

Amanda did not have any friends at school. Many times she felt that no one loved her or wanted to play with her, so she played alone. It is a good idea to be alone sometimes to think good thoughts about yourself, but it should not make you feel lonely and unloved like Amanda felt.

The children at school called Amanda ugly names while she was in the lunch line. They taunted* her with such remarks as "You have a hump nose! Your hair is like a horse's tail! Your eyes are like popcorn!" They even took her scarf off her head.

"I will tell the teacher," Amanda cried.

"Tell the teacher," they said. "Tell, go to jail." Don't forget your scarf. If you do, we don't care, we will pull out your hair."

Amanda pleaded, "Stop it, stop it! Leave me alone!"

The children hollered back, "Cry baby, cry baby!"

Amanda ran to her teacher and said, "The other children won't stop calling me ugly names or leave my scarf alone."

The teacher said, "Not again, Amanda! You are always complaining. Stay after school!"

A few minutes later, the teacher changed her mind and said to Amanda, "Stay in line! You don't have to stay after school."

*<u>Taunted</u> means **teased**.

On the way home from school every day, Amanda would walk past Mrs. Pierce's house. Mrs. Pierce was always sitting on her front porch at that time of day, and she would watch the children go by. When Amanda passed Mrs. Pierce's house, she would always say, "Good evening, Mrs. Pierce." But not this day. The children at school had given Amanda a very hard time by calling her names and pulling her scarf off her head.

When Amanda passed by Mrs. Pierce's house, she was crying uncontrollably.* She couldn't even stop crying to give Mrs. Pierce her usual greeting. Mrs. Pierce called to Amanda and said, "What is wrong, dear?"

"Nothing," Amanda sobbed.

Mrs. Pierce continued, her heart going out to Amanda. "Please, Amanda, tell me what is wrong. You are such a beautiful person. Why are you crying?"

Amanda walked up to the porch and said, "Today at school, while I was in the lunch line, some boys and girls laughed at me and said I had a hump nose, hair like a horse's tail, and eyes like pop-corn. They even pulled off my scarf. When I asked them to stop, they said, 'What are you going to do if we don't stop?'"

*<u>Uncontrollably</u> means **wildly, or out of control**.

Amanda continued. "When I told the teacher what had happened, she told me to leave the lunch line and to stay after school. But after a few moments, she changed her mind and said that I did not have to stay after school. I think she changed her mind because she does not like me and does not want me around."

Mrs. Pierce said sympathetically*, "I want you to learn to be happy, Amanda. Remember, you are a beautiful little girl!"

Amanda doubted Mrs. Pierce's kind words and blurted out, "No one loves me!"

Mrs. Pierce said, "Amanda, God loves you and I love you. However, you must love yourself first and learn how to be good to yourself."

Mrs. Pierce instructed Amanda to bring her the small hand mirror on the table and look into it. She asked, "What do you see?" "I see an ugly little girl!" Amanda answered.

Mrs. Pierce smiled and said quietly, "Well, I see a beautiful little girl and her name is Amanda! On Saturday, I would like you to come to a class I teach on how to build a good self-image."

"Oh, I don't know about that," Amanda hesitated*.

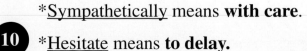

*Sympathetically means **with care**.

10 *Hesitate means **to delay**.

"Amanda, give me your mother's name and telephone number. I will call her and ask her permission," Mrs. Pierce continued.

"What did you say the class is about, Mrs. Pierce ?" Amanda asked.

Happy that she had caught Amanda's attention, Mrs. Pierce quickly answered, "The class is about learning how to build a good self-image."

"I'm not sure I know what that means," Amanda quipped*.

"Remember when you looked in the mirror and you thought you looked ugly? Well, after you come to my class, you will look in the mirror and you will see a beautiful little girl," Mrs. Pierce explained.

Amanda's eyes widened. "Mrs. Pierce, please call my mother as soon as you can. I want to see a beautiful Amanda when I look in the mirror," Amanda begged.

On the way home, Amanda started to feel sad again. She came home crying. Aiesha said to her, "If you were pretty like me, you would not be crying. Who would want to be like you?" Amanda didn't answer. She just walked to her room with a sad face. She threw herself on the bed and buried her head in her pillow.

Her mother knocked on her door and said, "Amanda, you are always crying. What are you crying about this time?"

*Quipped means **responded quickly and wittily.**

"Aiesha said that I am ugly!" Amanda shouted.

Amanda's mother said gently, "Amanda, you must learn to love yourself."

Amanda did not answer. She was thinking about how she could get the children at school to like her.

# Amanda Attends Mrs. Pierce's Class

Mrs. Pierce greeted the children and got right down to business by explaining the objectives* of her class.

The objectives were:

• To develop a good self-image

• To learn to think well of themselves and others

• To realize that each person is special

• To recognize the difference between a negative*
  (poor) self-image and a positive* (good) self-image

*<u>Objectives</u> means **goals**.

*<u>Negative</u> means **not pleasant**.

*<u>Positive</u> means **pleasant**.

# Learning The Meaning Of Self-Image

Mrs. Pierce then explored the meaning of self-image. We are all given talents by the Intelligence* that we must learn to develop. She explained that the **self** is you. **Image** is a picture. **Self-image** is the picture you have of yourself in your mind's eye. Your mind's eye is inside your head. As an example, she asked, "Has anyone ever imagined seeing a beautiful toy?"

"Yes!" the students answered.

"This means that you were using your imagination," said Mrs. Pierce. "You saw the toy with your mind's eye!"

"When you imagine yourself as a beautiful and intelligent person, you are seeing yourself with a good self-image."

"Now that you know the meaning of a good self-image," continued Mrs. Pierce, "I want each of you to tell me how you see yourself in the mirror and in your mind's eye."

16

*Intelligence in this context means the **power that works within a person as well as outside. It causes things to happen.**

"I see an ugly girl," Amanda said.   "I feel sad inside," Sharah said.

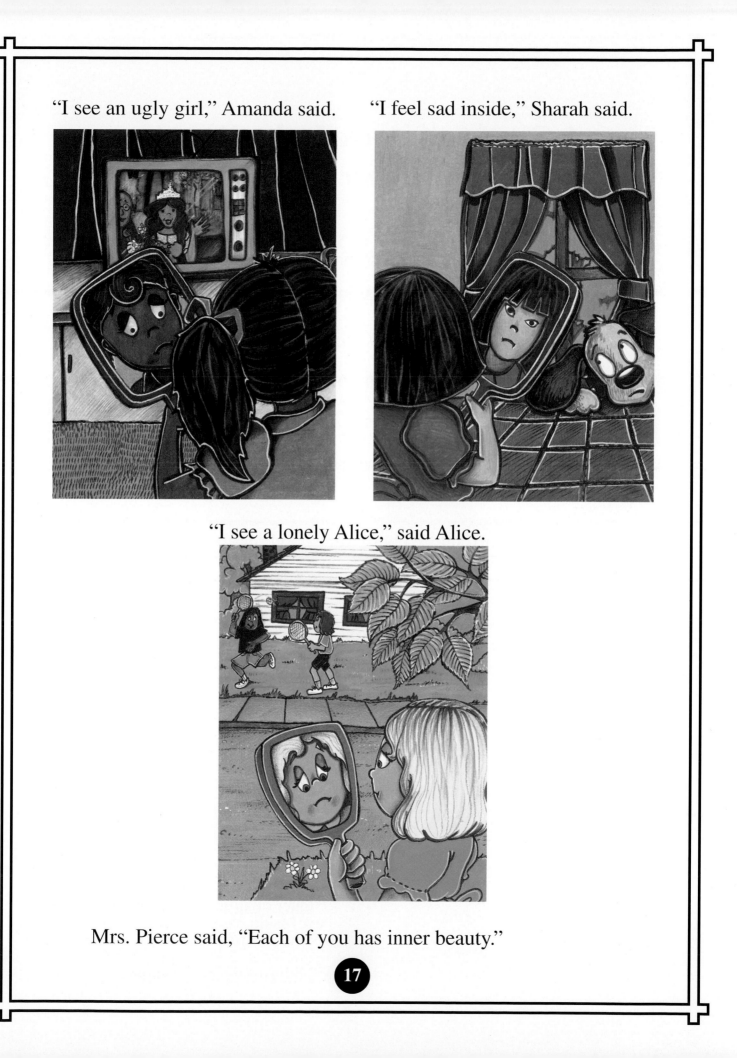

"I see a lonely Alice," said Alice.

Mrs. Pierce said, "Each of you has inner beauty."

# A Good Self-image Helps You Have Good Inner Qualities*

"All boys and girls have something good in them. You must learn to see the 'good' within yourself," said Mrs. Pierce.

"What good do we have within us?" Amanda asked.

"Dears, I want the three of you to think of one good thing you have within you," said Mrs. Pierce.

Alice thought for a moment and then proudly said, "I am honest."

Sharah firmly said, "I have very good manners."

Amanda was not as enthusiastic* as the others. Her mind was filled with questions. She quietly uttered, "I don't have any good inner qualities in me."

"Oh, yes you do have good in you!" shouted Alice. "Everyone does!"

*<u>Inner qualities</u> means the **way that you are inside**. Your true inner qualities should be **respectful, kind, and truthful.**

18 *<u>Enthusiastic</u> means **eager**.

Mrs. Pierce repeated what she had said earlier: "Each of you has an inner beauty."

"Let's make a list of all the good things that can be found within a person," Mrs. Pierce continued. "Love, kindness, intelligence, caring, politeness, and honesty are a few," she noted. "You all have these qualities within yourselves. Maybe you don't know that you have them, but you do!"

"What is intelligence*?" Sharah asked.

"Intelligence is the ability to think clearly and choose what is best for you," answered Mrs. Pierce. "For example, if a student chooses to read several books in six weeks, that is an intelligent choice."

Mrs. Pierce continued with her lesson and told the children that she would be asking them three questions. Then they would write a list of answers suggested together.

*Intelligence in this context means **thinking clearly, making good choices**, and **using reasoning**.

The questions were:

1. Do you know who you are?

2. Do you have a good self-image?

3. Do you look good to yourself?

The group's answers were:

1. Yes, I am a special person.

2. Yes, I have a good self-image.

3. Yes, I am beautiful.

Mrs. Pierce emphasized* the following:

Self-image is how you see yourself in the mirror. When you look

in the mirror, you must like the image you see.

 *Emphasized means **showed** that something is **important**.

"Remember children, your mind has a mirror just like the one on your dresser. You see your self-image in the mirror of your mind. If you see a beautiful self-image and you have good thoughts of yourself, you will also be happy. You should always see a very smart person," Mrs. Pierce said.

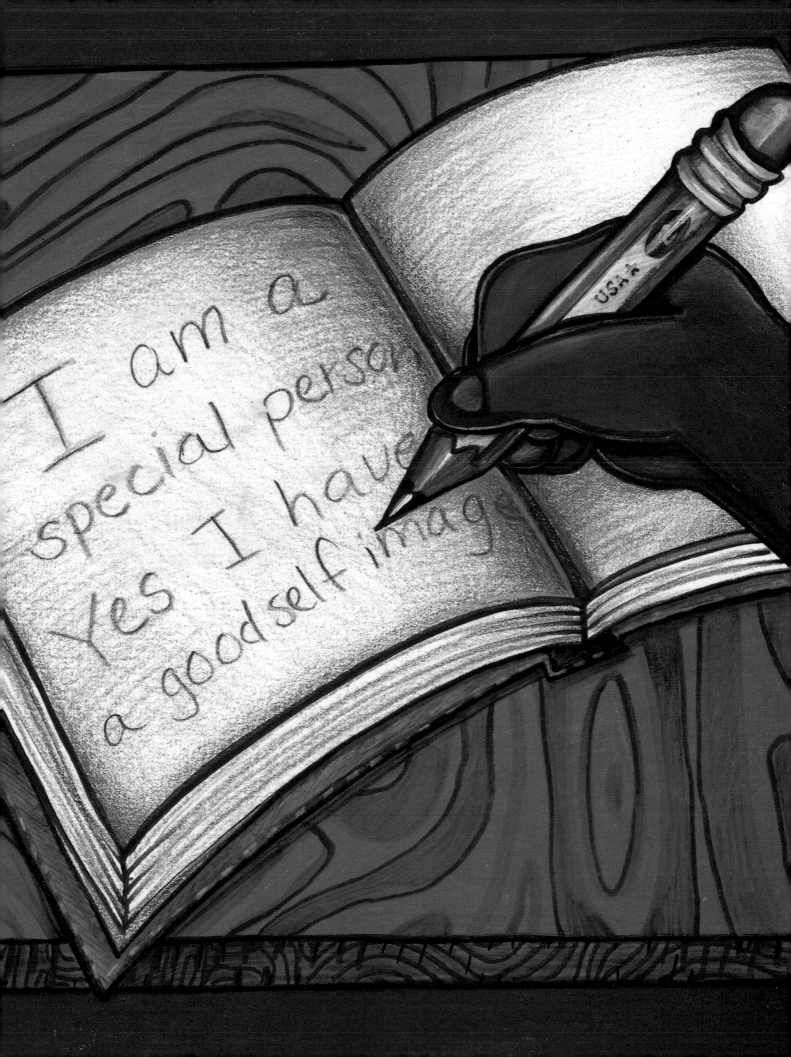

# How To See Your Self-Image In Your Mind's Eye

"Let's close our eyes now. First, picture a tree with green leaves. The tree is sitting on a hill covered with green grass. The leaves are blowing in the wind. The birds are singing. All is peaceful."

Then Mrs. Pierce instructed the children to open their eyes. She asked, "Did you see this tree with your two eyes?"

One child quickly spoke, "No, Mrs. Pierce, we saw this tree with our mind's eye."

"That's right, children," Mrs. Pierce said. "There is a way to see things other than just with your two eyes."

Mrs. Pierce explained to the children that they had used their mind's eyes to see some things in their imagination. She added that this is how we all see ourselves when we are not looking in the mirror.

"Now, close your eyes and picture yourself in your mind's eye as a smart person," said Mrs. Pierce.

"I see a very smart person in my mind's eye," Sharah said.

"This is the mental image you have of yourself," Mrs. Pierce continued. "Always try to see a smart and beautiful or handsome picture of yourself in your mind's eye. Always remember that your self-image is the way you see yourself in your mind's eye. It also tells how you feel about yourself, and what your life will be like."

Alice blurted out, "I want a good life, I want a good education, I want a good family, and I want to earn a good living."

"Well, Alice, we can set the stage for our own lives," Mrs. Pierce explained. Your mind has a mirror just like the one on a dresser. This is called your 'mind's eye.' If you like what you see, you feel good inside."

"Mrs. Pierce, what if negative thoughts enter my mind? What will happen?" Alice asked worriedly*.

"It will become real if you think about it long enough," said Mrs. Pierce. "But you have the power to turn negative thoughts into positive ones by thinking and acting on the opposite*."

Mrs. Pierce explained further, "For example, if you think you cannot do math, then you will not do math well. So, you can change that negative thought into a positive one by thinking, "I am a good math student and I work with my math daily."

26

*Worriedly means with **worried feelings.**
*Opposite means completely **different.**

"A good self-image can help you believe that you can learn anything you desire*, and that you can work toward acquiring* it.

"All boys and girls must have good self-images to grow up happy and healthy. Our mind's eye is inside of our heads, and we must use it to its fullest."

"If I see myself as a beautiful, well-educated person, will I eventually obtain a good education?" Sharah asked.

"Absolutely*! Whatever you want in life, learn to see yourself doing it, and then work for it," Mrs. Pierce answered. "For example, if you want to be a math teacher, you must see yourself working with math every day, listening to your teacher, and doing all of your homework. This is very important to remember. When you perform this experiment, you will learn a great deal about your self-image."

"Mrs. Pierce, I am beginning to see myself as a happier person, and I am feeling better about myself," said Amanda.

"That is wonderful, Amanda," Mrs. Pierce said. "Children, let's give Amanda a round of applause. A good self-image will help you identify how you feel about yourselves." The children smiled and clapped for Amanda.

Mrs. Pierce emphasized that the way you see yourself is the way others will see you. Inner feelings are shown in attitudes and behavior.

*Desire means **want.**
*Acquiring means **getting.**
*Absolutely means **perfect.**

Mrs. Pierce asked, "Do you know what positive attitudes are?"

"Yes," answered Alice.

Mrs. Pierce asked Alice to explain it to the others. "We can demonstrate* positive attitudes by showing kindness, smiling, sharing, and being polite," Alice said.

"Remember, we can all have either beautiful pictures or pictures that aren't so beautiful in our mind's eyes. But you must always work very hard to have a beautiful mental picture of yourself," said Mrs. Pierce.

"You must tell yourself five important things to keep your self-image positive:

1. I have a good self-image.

2. I see myself as a beautiful human being.

3. I love and respect myself.

4. I am honest and fair in everything I do.

5. I want the very best for myself."

Mrs. Pierce told the children they should say these five things to themselves every day.

*Demonstrate means to **show to others**.

# Feeling Good About Yourself and Your Family

Mrs. Pierce instructed the children to close their eyes and to think about how they feel when they are around someone they like very much.

"Maybe you are thinking of your mother, an aunt, a sister, or a brother, or just someone you like," said Mrs. Pierce.

"I feel good when I am around my family," said Alice.

"I think maybe my family likes me," Amanda said.

"Amanda, of course your family likes you," said Sharah. "But I know that sometimes families fuss at one another."

"When you share a caring relationship with someone, you feel happy and warm inside. You feel loved. When you feel loved, you enjoy doing good things to help others. We call this kindness," Mrs. Pierce continued. Mrs. Pierce asked the children to close their eyes again and, this time, to think of love and kindness. Then she asked them to think of a food they liked to eat.

"Can you see the color of your favorite food? Are you able to hear how it sounds when you bite into it?" Mrs. Pierce asked. "Now change the mental images in your mind's eye from the food that you like to a person you were kind to. The mental image* should be clear in your mind's eye," Mrs. Pierce said.

**30** *Mental image means a **picture** you see in your **mind's eye.**

Mrs. Pierce said that it can help to visualize physical features: What colors are their hair and eyes? How tall are they?

She explained that all of this is going on inside your mind while your eyes are closed.

"You can do this because you are using your imagination. Using your imagination is part of intelligence," Mrs. Pierce explained. "See! You do have love, kindness, and intelligence. These are good inner qualities, and you have them inside of you."

"I did not know that we had all of these beautiful inner qualities," said Amanda.

"Now you know! Your inner beauty is something you cannot see, touch, or smell. Your inner beauty is made up of intelligence, love, kindness, caring, and sharing. When we make good choices about our lives, we are using our inner beauty," said Mrs. Pierce.

*If you are reading this book with your family or friends, discuss the following\*:*

    *1. Where is your mind's eye?*

    *2. When you close your eyes, what do you see?*

    *3. How do you use your imagination?*

    *4. How will you show your intelligence?*

    *5. How will you show respect?*

 \*See answers on page 32.

# *Seeing Your Beautiful Self In The Mirror*

"When you look in the mirror, say to yourself, 'I see my beautiful face, I love myself, I am smart, and I am polite.' The more you love yourself, the more you will learn and do great things. You can be a nurse, lawyer, teacher, doctor, businessman, or businesswoman. You can become anything you want to be when you love yourself and work toward your goals," Mrs. Pierce emphasized. "For example, if you want good grades, think, listen, respect yourself, your teachers, and complete all of your homework assignments. And always remember that there are people in your life who love you and want to listen to you."

1. *Inside your head.*
2. *Your own self-image.*
3. *To visualize yourself or things.*
4. *By making good choices.*
5. *By being polite to others.*

## Amanda Was Grateful For Mrs. Pierce's Class On Building Her Self-Image

The day Amanda returned to school was a beautiful day. Her teacher said, "Amanda, I notice you are very happy. Is there something new and good in your life?"

"I am very happy since I have been taking classes from Mrs. Pierce on how to build a good self-image. She taught me to love myself and to see the good within myself first."

Amanda is now very happy with her self-image. She does not accept what others say or think about her. She has self-confidence. She works well with her teachers and they are very helpful to her.

Remember Amanda's sister, Aiesha? Aiesha was not kind to Amanda, but after Amanda learned to like herself and have self-confidence, she taught Aiesha to do the same. Now Aiesha is kind to everyone.

*Amanda lived happily.*

# GLOSSARY

## INCLUDING A SENTENCE FOR EACH GLOSSARY WORD

**Acquiring** means **getting**--*Acquiring a positive self-image is very important.*

**Absolutely** means **perfect.**

**Creator** means the **one who makes** things.  It is another name for **God**--*Mrs. Pierce believes that we are all born with good things which are gifts from the **Creator**.*

**Demonstrate** means to **show to others**--*Amanda knew how to **demonstrate** a positive attitude.*

**Desire** means **want**--*All people **desire** positive self-images.*

**Emphasized** means **showed** that something is **important**--*Mrs. Pierce wanted Amanda to feel good about herself so she **emphasized** ways to have a good self-image.*

**Enthusiastic** means **eager**--*At the beginning of the class, it seemed the other children were more **enthusiastic** about the class than Amanda was.*

**Inner Qualities** means the **way that you are inside**.  Your true inner qualities are to be **respectful, kind, and truthful**--*Mrs. Pierce wanted Amanda to let her inner qualities shine through.*

**Intelligence** means **thinking clearly, making good choices**, and **using reasoning**--*Mrs. Pierce taught Amanda how to be **intelligent** by using her intelligence and making good choices.*

**Mental image** means a **picture** of a thing one holds in his or her **mind**--*Mrs. Pierce taught Amanda how to see a beautiful **mental image** of herself.*

**Objectives** means **goals**--*Mrs. Pierce's class had important **objectives**.*

**Opposite** means completely **different**--*positive is the **opposite** of negative.*

**Positive** means **pleasant**--*Mrs. Pierce taught Amanda how to have a positive self-image.*

**Negative** means **unpleasant**--*Mrs. Pierce taught Amanda how not to see a **negative** mental image of herself.*

**Sympathetically** means **with care**--*Mrs. Pierce spoke to Amanda **sympathetically**.*

**Taunted** means **teased**--*The children made Amanda sad because they **taunted** her.*

**Uncontrollably** means **wildly** or out of control--*The children hurt Amanda's feelings until she cried **uncontrollably**.*

**Worriedly** means with **worried feelings**--*Amanda asked **worriedly** about negative thoughts.  Mrs. Pierce let her know that she had the power to change negative thoughts into positive thoughts.*

*Other books by the same author:* Will be published, 1999

1.  *Granny and My Five Senses* Children need to learn to appreciate their five senses. Then they will be more open to new and greater ideas.

2.  *Granny and My Mind* When a child becomes aware of his or her mind and its potential, she or he will work more to develop it.

3. *Granny Talks About The Hidden Sense* Children need to become more aware of their hidden sense for protection. This book will help raise their awareness of their feelings of danger.

4. *Granny and My Dream* The granddaughter's dreams about Granny in the library surrounded by hundreds of books on love. Will raise awareness in children about the importance of love and respect.

5. *Granny, the Wise Teacher* Granny tells a story about how ants prepare for winter.

6.  *Love and Respect in the Family* Love and respect are missing in many homes today. Reading this book alone or with family members will help to bring love and respect within the family, in school, and in the community.

7. *The Importance of Living in Harmony* Harmony is missing in many homes today. We want to put harmony back into the home. If you and your family read this book, it will help you to create harmony within yourselves, home, and community.

8. *Amanda's Poor Self-Image* Children will feel more secure with a good self-image. This book will help your child to reach this important stage of self-development.

9. *Multi-Ethics Kit* For 1st and 2nd grades, these books explore concepts such as harmony, respect, self-control, self-image, self-awareness, thinking before speaking, listening skills, positive motivation, communication skills, and other subjects that are important to the healthy development of young people. This kit includes exercises, transparencies, and a detailed instruction manual. It is the first part of the Self-Awareness Curriculum Series.

10. *Self-Awareness Curriculum* These books are for grades 3 through 10. They make up the second level of the Self-Awareness Curriculum Series. This level also covers social issues, such as drugs/alcohol, AIDS, and suffering from loss.

11. *Parent Companion Manual* The PCM is an important component of the Self-Awareness Curriculum. The PCM has been developed to raise parents' awareness of the critical need for their own involvement in their children's education.

**Send a money order to:** **The Victory & Freedom Books Publishing, Inc.**

**P.O. Box 2517, Stone Mountain , GA 30386.**
*Call or Fax (770) 987-3111*